For Celia
—J. C.

For Henry,
Christopher,
and Emma —G. P.

Published in the United States
of America in 2008 by
Walker Publishing Company, Inc.

Distributed to the trade by
Macmillan

For information about permission to reproduce
selections from this book, write to Permissions,
Walker & Company, 175 Fifth Avenue,
New York, New York 10010

Library of Congress Cataloging-in-Publication Data
Clarke, Jane.
Stuck in the mud / Jane Clarke ; illustrations by
Garry Parsons.
p.   cm.
Summary: In this cumulative, rhyming story,
a little chick needs help from all his farmyard
friends to get out of the mud.
ISBN-13: 978-0-8027-9758-2 •
ISBN-10: 0-8027-9758-X
[1. Mud—Fiction. 2. Chickens—Fiction.
3. Animals—Infancy—Fiction. 4. Domestic
animals—Fiction. 5. Rescues—Fiction.
6. Stories in rhyme.] I. Parsons, Garry, ill.
II. Title.
PZ8.3.C5484St 2008
[E]—dc22
2007032179

All papers used by Walker & Company
are natural, recyclable products made from
wood grown in well-managed forests. The
manufacturing processes conform to the
environmental regulations of the country
of origin.

Visit Walker & Company's Web site
at www.walkeryoungreaders.com
Printed in China
2 4 6 8 10 9 7 5 3

Typeset in Betabet Black and Clubhouse
Art created with acrylics

Stuck
in the
Mud

Jane Clarke

Illustrations by Garry Parsons

Walker & Company
New York

Early in the morning,
down on the farm,
a new day was dawning,
peaceful and calm.

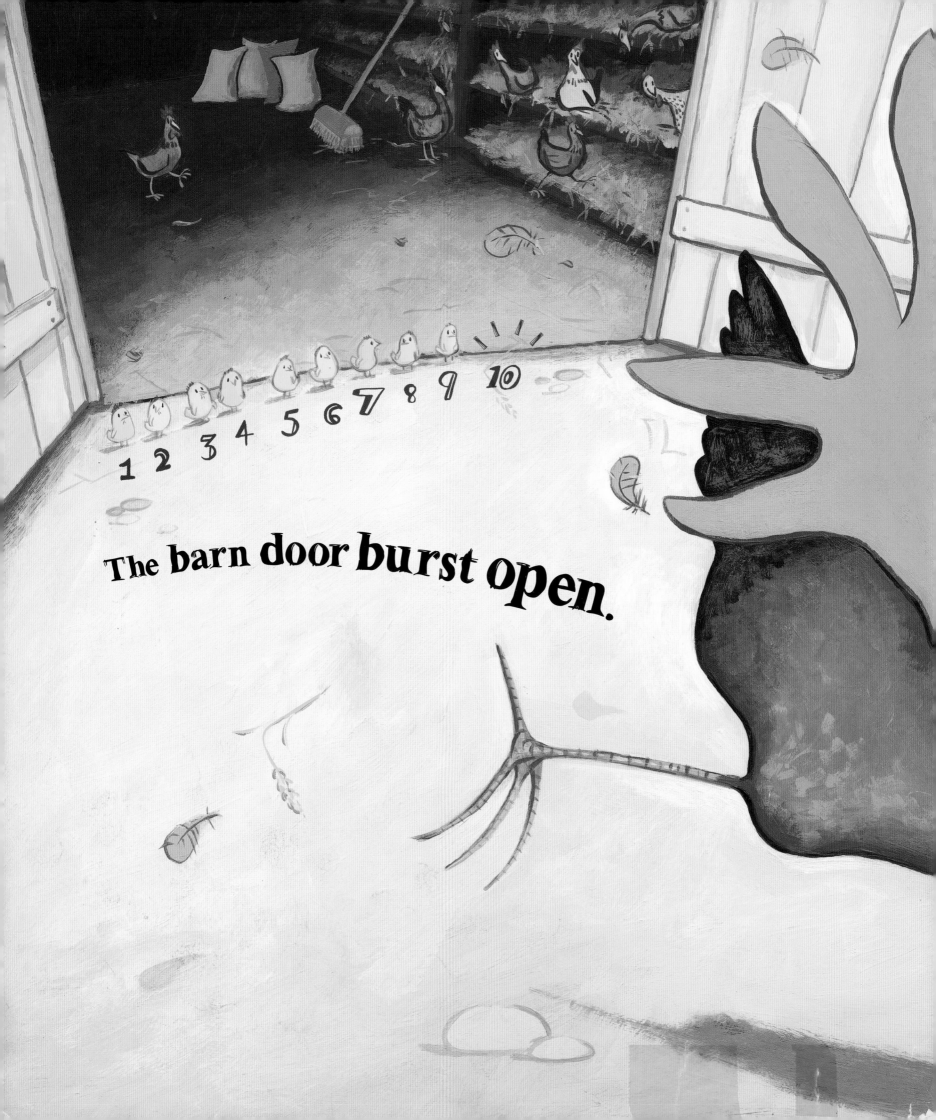

The barn door burst open.

"Help! Help!" clucked the hen.

"My poor little **chick!**

He's **stuck** in the **mud** . . .

and the mud's
deep and **thick!**

. . . and now
I'm **stuck** too,"
said the poor muddy hen.

Cat heard
the hen.

"Hold on,
wait for me!
It's **purr-fectly** easy.
I'll soon
pull you free."

Cluck!
Cluck!
Cluck!

Cat **pushed** and
she **p u l l e d**
again and again . . .

. . . but soon **she was stuck** with the poor muddy hen.

Dog heard
the cat.

"I'll help you!"

he yapped.

Meow!

So he jumped in the mud,
and he got his paws
trapped.

Dog **pushed** and
he **p u l l e d**
again and again . . .

. . . but soon he was **stuck**
with the cat and the hen.

Sheep heard
the dog . . .

Woof!
Woof!
Woof!

. . . and without even thinking,
she stepped in the mud,
and soon
she
was
sinking.

Sheep **pushed** and
she ***pulled***
again and again . . .

Cheep!

. . . but poor
Sheep was
stuck
with Dog,
Cat, and Hen!

Horse heard
the sheep.

Baa!

Horse **pushed** and
he **pulled**
again and again . . .

but then **he** was **stuck**
with Sheep, Dog, Cat, and Hen.

"What's this?"
said the farmer.
"Phew . . .

. . . this mud is smelly!
And now mucky mud

"is all over my belly!"

He **pushed** and he **p u l l e d** again and again . . .

. . . but the farmer
was **stuck**
with them all,
like the hen.

"Oh dear,"
said the chick . . .

"You **pushed** and
you **p u l l e d**
again and again,

but I'm not stuck now and I wasn't stuck then!

Mud is great fun!
I'm sure you'll agree.
I love mucky mud—

thanks for playing with me!"